Disnep • PIXAR

TOY STORY 2

Ladybird

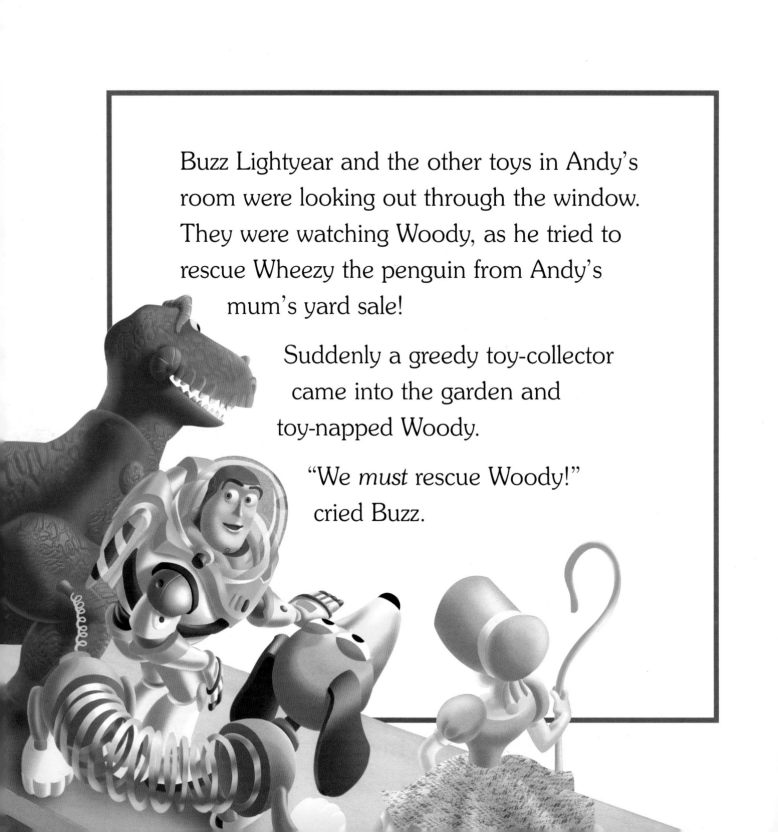

Buzz Lightyear and the other toys in Andy's room were looking out through the window. They were watching Woody, as he tried to rescue Wheezy the penguin from Andy's mum's yard sale!

Suddenly a greedy toy-collector came into the garden and toy-napped Woody.

"We *must* rescue Woody!" cried Buzz.

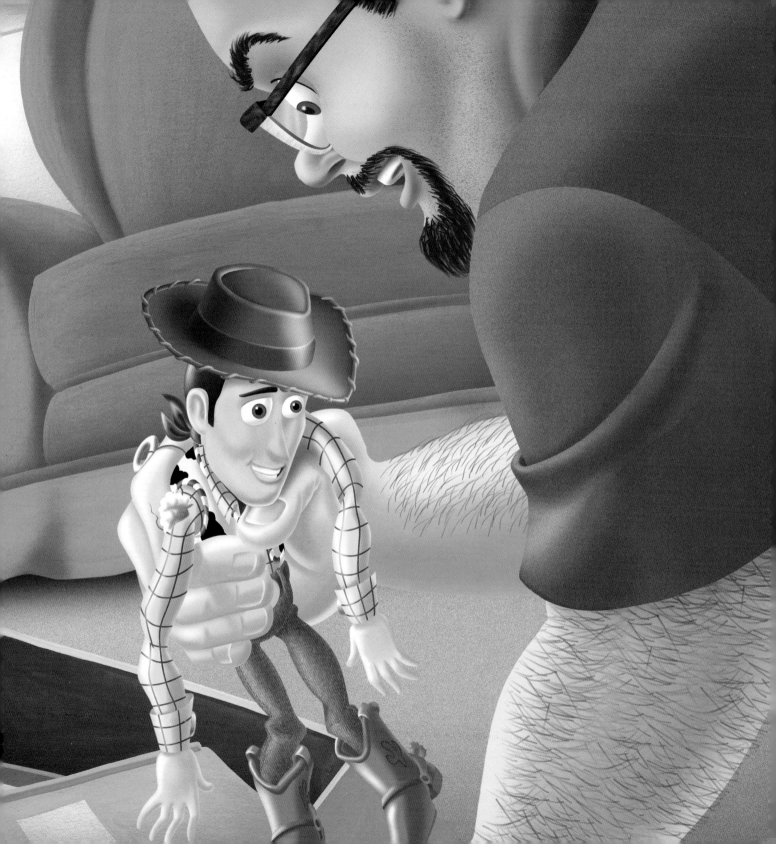

The toy-collector, whose name was Al, left Woody in his apartment.

Woody looked around. Suddenly he was surprised by Bullseye, a floppy little horse, and Jessie, a friendly cowgirl. "You're here at last!" they cried.

"Let's show you who you really are!" said Stinky Pete, an old prospector doll.

Jessie turned on the TV.

"It's Woody's Roundup!" said the TV announcer. Woody couldn't believe it! He had once been a television star, and now he was a collectable!

"And with you here," said Stinky Pete, "Al can sell us all to a museum in Japan."

It was amazing… but Woody didn't want to belong to a museum. All he wanted was to get back to Andy.

Meanwhile, the rescue mission had begun. "To Al's Toy Barn, and Beyond!" Buzz shouted bravely. The clever toys had worked out that Al owned the local toy shop. They thought that Woody would be there.

But Woody was still in Al's apartment. The toy collector looked at Woody and said, "You're going to make me rich, rich, ri…" RIPP! …the cowboy's arm came off in his hand. "Oh no!" gasped Al. "I'll have to get that repaired."

Not far away, Buzz and the rescue team were hiding under some traffic cones, trying to cross a busy road. Cars swerved all around them! The toys were almost across, when Mr Potato Head trod in some bubble gum…

At last he pulled his shoe loose and ran.

Ignoring the sound of horns and brakes behind them, the toys hurried inside Al's Toy Barn.

Up in the apartment, Woody's arm had been repaired. "I can go home to Andy now!" he smiled.

"But, Woody," said Jessie sadly, "if you go away, we'll have to go back into storage. And anyway even the greatest kids outgrow their toys," she sighed. Then she told him how her owner had grown up and given her away.

"Maybe you're right," Woody said thoughtfully. "Perhaps I will stay with you after all."

Just then, CRASH! Using Rex as a battering ram, Andy's toys smashed their way into Al's apartment. They'd followed all the clues and found Woody at last!

"Come on!" Buzz ordered quickly. "Let's get back to Andy."

But Woody didn't move. "I'm staying here," he said. And he turned on the TV. Andy's toys couldn't believe it! They walked slowly away without their friend.

"You've got a friend in me," sang the
TV Woody to a little boy on the screen.
It made Woody think of Andy, and the little
cowboy realised he'd made a big mistake.

"Buzz! Wait!" Woody shouted. But the
Prospector blocked the way.

"No one's going anywhere!"
he said grimly. "Except to
the museum!"

Just then, Al came in.

Buzz and his friends watched as Al packed
Woody and the other toys into a suitcase.
Soon he was ready to leave for the airport.

Andy's toys rushed to the lift. Stretching out
his coils, Slinky managed to reach the case and
open the catch. But the Prospector snatched
Woody out of reach, and then Al walked away.

The toys weren't beaten yet.
Mr Potato Head had a plan...

"Pizza anyone?" he asked,
pointing to a pizza delivery truck.
The toys cheered, jumped in
and drove to the airport.

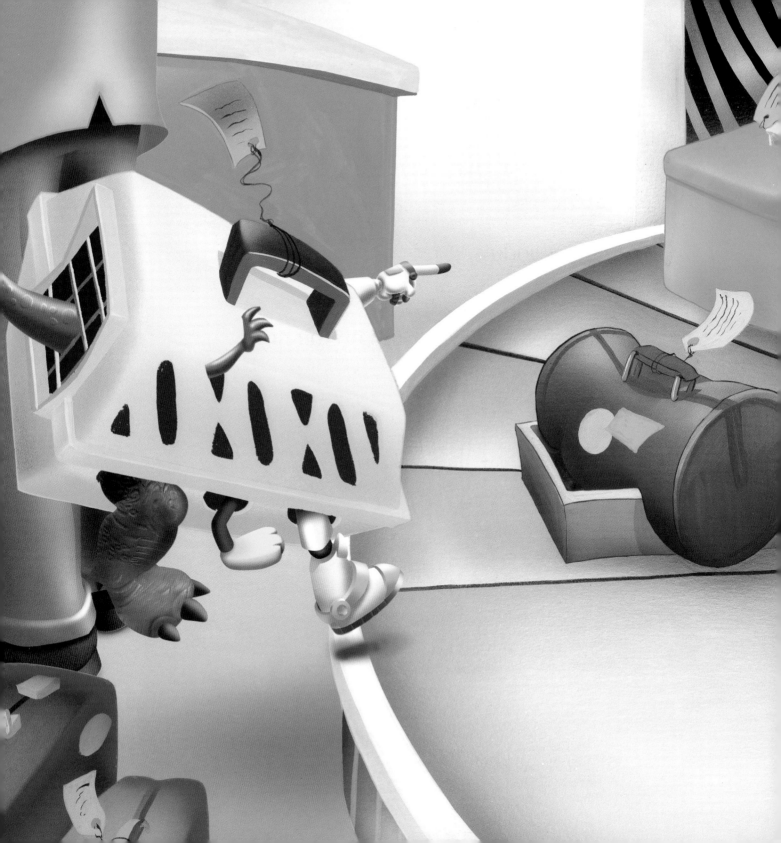

Moments later, they were scooting along the conveyor belt in a pet carrier.

"I think Woody's in this one!" cried Buzz, unlatching a suitcase.

POW! A fist punched Buzz on the nose. It was the Prospector. He started to attack Buzz.

Woody leapt out of the case to help his friend.
Together, they packed the old Prospector away
in a passing backpack.

Woody looked around. Bullseye was safe but
Jessie was still in the suitcase.

"Jessie deserves another chance to play with
someone who will love her,"
Woody thought.

With seconds to spare before
the plane started to move,
Woody grabbed Jessie.

They jumped safely down onto Bullseye's back, where Buzz was waiting for them. Then they all galloped back to their friends.

"YEEEEHAAAAH!" cried Woody triumphantly. His arm was torn off again, and they still had to find their way home. But soon they'd be back where they belonged – with Andy.